To all my favorite redheads
—S. L.

To my very supportive mother and father
—R. C.

· A NOTE ON THE STORY ·

When I was a little girl in the West, I used to visit my grandmother, who lived all by herself on a ranch near Red Rock, Arizona. And when I read the story of Little Red Riding Hood and her grandmother and the wolf, I was puzzled.

First of all, how could a girl go riding dressed like that? Flapping red capes scare horses. And second, *my* grandmother would never have allowed a wolf to lay a tooth on her—or any of us children. And finally, no real wolf would ever act like the wolf in the story, unless, as my grandmother would say, he'd been eating locoweed.

Henry Holt and Company, LLC
Publishers since 1866
175 Fifth Avenue
New York, New York 10010
www.HenryHoltKids.com

Henry Holt® is a registered trademark of Henry Holt and Company, LLC.
Text copyright © 1997 by Susan Lowell. Illustrations copyright © 1997 by Randy Cecil.
All rights reserved.
Distributed in Canada by H. B. Fenn and Company Ltd.

Library of Congress Cataloging-in-Publication Data
Lowell, Susan.
Little red cowboy hat / Susan Lowell; illustrations by Randy Cecil.
Summary: A Southwestern version of "Little Red Riding Hood" in which Little Red rides
her pony, Buck, to Grandma's ranch with a jar of cactus jelly in a saddlebag.
(1. Grandmothers—Fiction. 2. Wolves—Fiction. 3. Southwest, New—Fiction.) I. Cecil, Randy, ill. II. Title.
PZ7.F9648Li 1996 [E]—dc20 96-31201

ISBN-13: 978-0-8050-3508-7 / ISBN-10: 0-8050-3508-7 (hardcover)
5 7 9 10 8 6
ISBN-13: 978-0-8050-6483-4 / ISBN-10: 0-8050-6483-4 (paperback)
5 7 9 10 8 6
First published in hardcover in 1997 by Henry Holt and Company
First paperback edition—2000
Printed in China on acid-free paper. ∞

The artist used gouache on paper to create the illustrations for this book.

Little Red Cowboy Hat

SUSAN LOWELL

Illustrations by

RANDY CECIL

Henry Holt and Company · New York

NCE UPON A RANCH, far away in the wilds of the West, there lived a little girl with red, red hair. Her hair was a fine color somewhere between firecrackers and new pennies. And to top it off, her grandmother gave her a bright red cowboy hat.

So everybody called her Little Red Cowboy Hat, or Little Red for short.

One day her mother said, "Little Red, your grandma's sick in bed. Ride over there and take her this loaf of homemade bread and jar of cactus jelly."

"Yes, ma'am," said Little Red, who loved to visit her grandmother.

"Don't dillydally along the way," warned her mother.

"No, ma'am," said Little Red.

"And be careful," her mother said. "It's rattlesnake season."

"Yes, ma'am."

Little Red put her cowboy hat on her head and saddled her buckskin pony. She packed the loaf of bread and jar of jelly in her saddlebag. And then she set off for her grandmother's ranch several miles away.

First she rode down into a deep canyon. *Clink-clunk-crunch* went the pony's feet, striking sparks from the rocks.

Next she rode up onto a wide mesa where gold poppies and blue lupines blossomed in the grass.

"Grandma loves flowers," thought Little Red. "I'll just stop for a minute."

As she was picking wildflowers, she heard her pony give a snort.
"Whoa, Buck!" said Little Red, turning around.
"A snake?" she wondered.

Then she saw the wolf.

"Howdy, little girl," he said. He wore a cowboy hat three shades blacker than a locomotive.

"Hi," she said.

The wolf stood between her and the pony. She didn't want to talk to him, but she'd been raised to be polite.

"What's your name, honey?" he asked.

He came closer than she liked.

"Little Red Cowboy Hat," she answered reluctantly. She'd also been raised to tell the truth.

"Red?" said the wolf.

A creepy feeling ran up her backbone, and tingled in the roots of her hair.

"Red as in ... ketchup?" he asked. "Or red as in ... blood?"

She didn't answer. He was much too close. She could count the teeth in his smile.

"Where are you going, sugar?" he said. "Why not take a little ride with me?"

Just then the pony whinnied and reared.

"Whoa, Buck!" cried Little Red.

The wolf leaped away from Buck's hard hooves, and Little Red seized the reins and jumped safely into the saddle.

"To Grandma's house!" she shouted as she galloped away.

When Little Red reached her grandmother's ranch, she didn't hear a sound except the windmill creaking: *skree, skree.* The chickens didn't even cluck. Usually Grandma was outside, doctoring a cow or mixing cement. But now nothing moved except three buzzards circling high up in the sky.

"Poor Grandma!" thought Little Red.

She tied Buck to the hitching post and tippy-toed into the ranch house. It was as quiet as a tree full of owls.

"Grandma?" she called softly.

She saw a big lump in her grandmother's bed. The lacy edge of
Grandma's shower cap peeked out above the patchwork quilt.

"I brought you some bread and jelly, Grandma," said Little Red.

"Thank you, honey bun," said a muffled voice.

Thump!

What was that noise outside? Little Red stiffened. Something was wrong.

"Grandma," she said, "is that you?"

"Of course it is, sweetie."

"I can't see you," said Little Red suspiciously.

The lump moved. Deep down in the bedclothes, a strange dark eye
glittered.

"Shoot!" thought Little Red. "Grandma must be really sick."

"What big eyes you have, Grandma!" she said.

"The better to see you with, pumpkin," said the voice.

Ka-thump! came the noise outside again.

The quilt fell away from a huge, hairy muzzle. Now Little Red Cowboy Hat knew perfectly well that this was not her grandmother. But where *was* Grandma? She decided to string the wolf along until she found out.

So she went on bravely: "What a big nose you have, Grandma!"

"The better to smell you with, dumpling," said the figure in the bed.

Thump! Thump!

"And what sharp teeth you have, Grandma!"

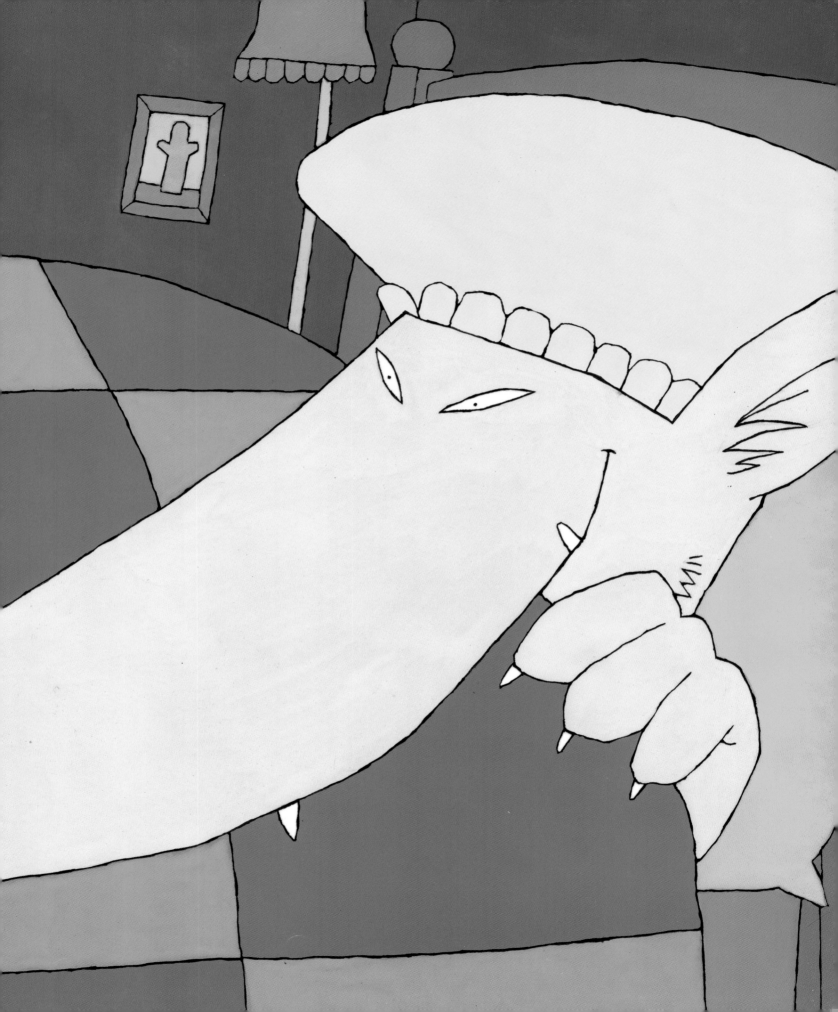

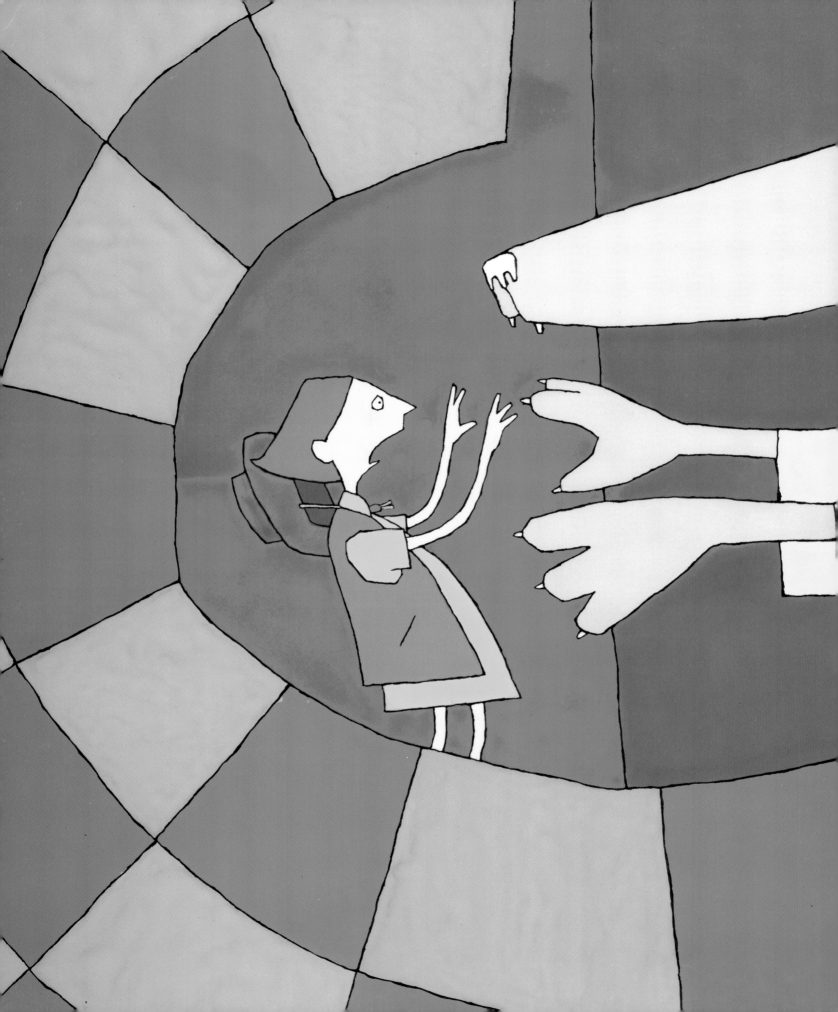

"The better to eat you with, angel pie!"
And the wolf sat bolt upright and
grabbed Little Red Cowboy Hat.
THUMP! THUMP! THUMP!
"Ow!" she screamed.
"Quiet, you delicious morsel," he snarled,
licking his chops.

"Oh, no you don't!" yelled a familiar voice. "Get your paws off her, you varmint!"

And there was Little Red Cowboy Hat's grandma, with an ax in her hand. She had been chopping wood. The wolf dropped Little Red like a hot potato and made a break for the window.

"Are you all right, Red?" called Grandma.

"Yes, ma'am!"

The wolf tripped over his nightgown, and then he got stuck in the window. His tail waved helplessly behind him. Meanwhile, Grandma snatched her shotgun from the mantel.

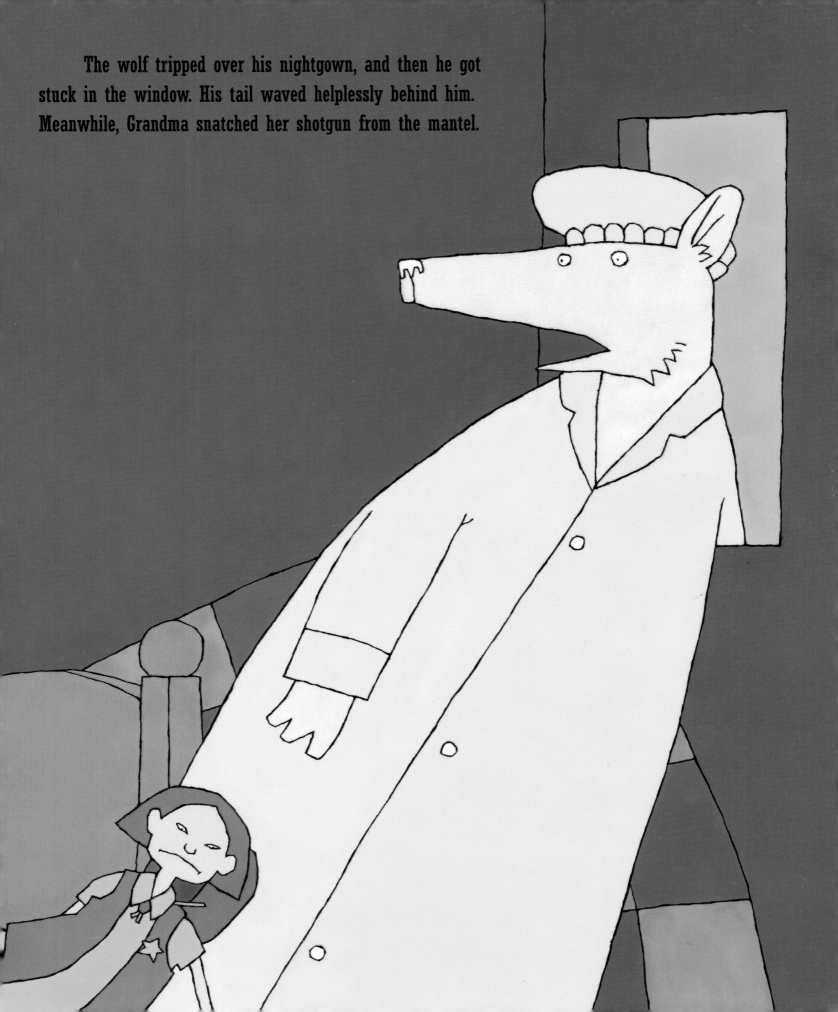

POW!

"Take that, you low-life lobo!" she shouted. "Come on, Red!"

Little Red leaped onto Buck and twirled her lasso. Together they chased the wolf down the road.

"Tut-tut-tut!" cried the chickens.

"Nnoo! Nnnooo!" called the cattle.

"Breaking into my house!" puffed Grandma.

POW!   "Wearing my clothes!"   *KA-BLAM!*

"Getting fleas in my bed!"

POW! BAM!

"Messing with my granddaughter!"

SWISH! BOOM!

"You'd look mighty good as a rug, Mister Wolf!"

SPLAT!

Later, back at the ranch, Little Red Cowboy Hat and her grandma sat down to eat their bread and cactus jelly.

"Now, Red, have you learned your lesson?" asked Grandma.

"Yep. A girl's gotta stick up for herself," said Little Red.

Her windblown hair glowed in the light of the setting sun. It was a fine color somewhere between autumn leaves and chili peppers, and Grandma smiled as she smoothed it down.

"That yellow-bellied, snake-blooded, skunk-eyed, rancid son of a parallelogram!" she said. "This time he picked the wrong grandma."

And they never had any wolf trouble around her ranch again.